Bubble, Bubble, Bubble, Splash!

to the melody of "The Ants Go Marching One by One"

by Megan Fitzharris

Bubble, Bubble, Bubble, Splash!

Written by Megan Fitzharris
Illustrated by Brianna Camp
Edited by Frank Monahan

PUBLISHED BY

For my sons.

I love you more than anything in the whole wide world.

The fish are swimming one by one, hurrah, hurrah!
The fish are swimming one by one, hurrah, hurrah!
The fish are swimming one by one,
the Little One says come join the fun
And they all swim quickly
Down to the reef
To get away from the sharks
Bubble, bubble, bubble...

The fish are swimming two by two, hurrah, hurrah!
The fish are swimming two by two, hurrah, hurrah!
The fish are swimming two by two,
the Little One swims into the deep, deep blue,
And they all swim quickly
Down to the reef
To get away from the sharks
Bubble, bubble, bubble...

The fish are swimming three by three, hurrah, hurrah!
The fish are swimming three by three, hurrah, hurrah!
The fish are swimming three by three,
the Little One sees a sea anemone,
And they all swim quickly
Down to the reef
To get away from the sharks
Bubble, bubble, bubble...

The fish are swimming four by four, hurrah, hurrah!
The fish are swimming four by four, hurrah, hurrah!
The fish are swimming four by four,
the Little One plays on the sandy floor,
And they all swim quickly
Down to the reef
To get away from the sharks
Bubble, bubble, bubble...

The fish are swimming five by five, hurrah, hurrah!
The fish are swimming five by five, hurrah, hurrah!
The fish are swimming five by five,
the Little One watches a turtle dive,
And they all swim quickly
Down to the reef
To get away from the sharks
Bubble, bubble, bubble...

The fish are swimming six by six, hurrah, hurrah!
The fish are swimming six by six, hurrah, hurrah!
The fish are swimming six by six,
the Little One practices her fin kicks,
And they all swim quickly
Down to the reef
To get away from the sharks
Bubble, bubble, bubble...

The fish are swimming seven by seven, hurrah, hurrah!
The fish are swimming seven by seven, hurrah, hurrah!
The fish are swimming seven by seven,
the Little One flits through coral heaven,
And they all swim quickly
Down to the reef
To get away from the sharks
Bubble, bubble, bubble...

The fish are swimming eight by eight, hurrah, hurrah!
The fish are swimming eight by eight, hurrah, hurrah!
The fish are swimming eight by eight,
the Little One passes a smooth sea skate.
And they all swim quickly
Down to the reef
To get away from the sharks
Bubble, bubble, bubble...

The fish are swimming nine by nine, hurrah, hurrah!
The fish are swimming nine by nine, hurrah, hurrah!
The fish are swimming nine by nine,
the Little One hides as reef sharks dine.
'Cause they all swam quickly
Down to the reef
To get away from the sharks
Bubble, bubble, bubble…

The fish are swimming ten by ten, hurrah, hurrah!
The fish are swimming ten by ten, hurrah, hurrah!
The fish are swimming ten by ten,
the Little One jumps in the waves again,
As they all swim quickly
Up to the top
Where the waves move and crash,
Bubble, bubble, bubble, SPLASH!

18

Glossary

The Real World of *Bubble, Bubble, Bubble, Splash!*

1. Coral Reef

A coral reef is an underwater ecosystem formed by coral polyps. The coral polyps are organisms that live in large groups called colonies. These colonies create hard structures that help form the reef where thousands of plants and animals live. There are different types of corals, which create different shapes and can live up to hundreds of years. Sadly, due to human pollution, warmer global temperatures, too much fishing, and more, coral reefs are endangered. This means that they are at risk of being destroyed and could become extinct, just like the dinosaurs. As a

Coral Reef: U.S. Fish & Wildlife Service - Pacific Region's Photo credit: Jim Maragos/U.S. Fish and Wildlife Service, CC BY 2.0 <https://creativecommons.org/licenses/by/2.0>, via Wikimedia Commons

home to more than 25% of all the ocean life on our planet, this would be a horrible tragedy. All of the corals that are highlighted in this book are threatened. We must work to respect and preserve all life, including coral reefs on our planet.

2. Boulder star coral

Boulder star coral along with other star corals, elkhorn corals, and staghorn corals built the Caribbean coral reefs over the past 5,000 years! Boulder star corals usually form big clumps with bumpy surfaces or sometimes plates. They can be orange, green or greyish brown with pale or white edges.

Boulder star coral: LASZLO ILYES from Cleveland, Ohio, USA, CC BY 2.0 <https://creativecommons.org/licenses/by/2.0>, via Wikimedia Commons

3. Elkhorn coral

Elkhorn corals only exist in the Caribbean and Western Atlantic Ocean. They grow in tight groups called "thickets" that provide habitat, or housing, for many different animals in shallow water. It used to be the most common type of coral in the Caribbean reefs, but disease has killed off more than 97% of it in the last 30 years.

Paul Asman and Jill Lenoble, CC BY2.0 <https://creativecommons.org/licenses/by/2.0>, via Wikimedia Commons

4. Blue Chromis
Grows to 5 inches/12.7 centimeters

Blue chromis like to swim in schools of 6 or more fish. When they are mating, the male fish creates a nest in the sand and watches over the eggs the female lays until they hatch. Blue chromis eat plankton, tiny organisms that float in the ocean water.

Brian Gratwicke, CC BY 2.0 <https://creativecommons.org/licenses/by/2.0>, via Wikimedia Commons

5. Foureye Butterflyfish
Grows to 6 in/15.24 cm

The foureye butterflyfish is a flat fish with a dark spot by its tail. The dark spot confuses predators by making it hard to see which way the fish is swimming. They are great swimmers who can move sideways or even upside down.

LASZLO ILYES from Cleveland, Ohio, USA, CC BY 2.0 <https://creativecommons.org/licenses/by/2.0>, via Wikimedia Commons

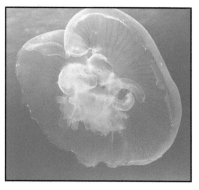

Moon Jellyfish
Grows to 10-16 in/25-40 cm

Moon jellyfish have very round, white bodies that are quite transparent or see through. They do not have a brain and only about 5% of their body is solid. Moon jellyfish drift where the water will carry them, and they eat by stinging prey with its tentacles and pulling it whole into its stomach.

6. Reef Squirrelfish
Grows to 5.9 in/14.98 cm

Reef squirrelfish have spiny fins and rough scales. They are nocturnal, which means they eat and play at night. They hide in the reef during the day.

7. Sea Anemone

Sea anemones are a group of animals that have stinging tentacles that reach out to stun their food or ward off predators. There are more than 1,100 types of sea anemones in the world and they can live up to 50 years. The two sea anemones highlighted in this book only exist in the Caribbean Sea and the western Atlantic Ocean.

8. Giant Caribbean Sea Anemone
Grows to 16 in/40 cm around and 6 in/15.24 cm high

A very large sea anemone, the Giant Caribbean Sea Anemone has the ability to slowly crawl to find the best location for finding food on the reef. They will protect their position on the reef to ensure they can have good food.

9. American Warty Anemone *Grows to 1.6 in/4 cm around and .6 in/1.5 cm high*

A nocturnal anemone, the American Warty Anemone opens and extends its tentacles at night to catch food and closes up into a blob shape during the day.

10. Balloonfish (Spiny porcupinefish) *Grows to 14 in/35.56 cm*

Spiny porcupinefish or balloonfish can puff up their bodies when they are in danger. They can make themselves look 3 times bigger than usual. They also have long spines that lay flat along their bodies. When they inflate like a balloon, the spines stick out like a porcupine which helps discourage predators.

Linnaea Mallette (publicdomainpictures.net)

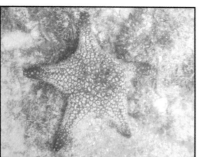

11. Cushion Star *Grows to 19.6 in/50 cm*

A cushion star is a species of starfish that gets its name from its puffed-up appearance. Cushion stars may have 4, 5, or 6 arms. To eat, they will send their stomachs out of their mouths to consume their prey and then pull it back in.

Steve Ryan, CC BY-SA 2.0 <https://creativecommons.org/licenses/by-sa/2.0>, via Wikimedia Commons

12. Smooth Trunkfish *Grows to 19 inches/48.26 cm*

The smooth trunkfish is a member of the boxfish family, fish that have square shaped bodies. It is a slow swimmer who most often swims alone. It eats benthic invertebrates or small creatures that live in the sandy bottom of the ocean. It uncovers them by shooting a jet stream of water out of its mouth to uncover them.

Kris Mikael Krister: https://commons.m.wikimedia.org/wiki/
File:Smooth_Trunkfish_Lactophrys_Triqueter_(252728203).jpeg

13. Hawksbill Sea Turtle *Grows to 35 in/90 cm*

The hawksbill sea turtle grows as large as 150 lbs. and can live a very long life, up to 100 years. The turtle's favorite food are sea sponges which live on coral reefs; they eat an average of 1,200 lbs of sponges a year. However, hawksbill sea turtles are endangered due to human interference and loss of coral reef habitat.

DRVIP93, CC BY-SA 4.0 <https://creativecommons.org/licenses/by-sa/4.0>, via Wikimedia Commons

14. Sergeant Major Damselfish *Grows to 9 in/22.9 cm*

The sergeant major damselfish is one of many different kinds of damselfish, easily recognizable by its black and white stripes. Female sergeant major damselfish choose a mate by watching the males do a "signal jump." The male fish swim very fast up and then back down, making a pulse sound under the water.

15. Caribbean Reef Octopus *Mantle grows to 24 in/60 cm*

The Caribbean reef octopus is one of the most intelligent invertebrates, animals without backbones, in the world. They can hide themselves perfectly by changing their color to match whatever is around them. They can even change their skin and muscles to look like the texture of the coral they are sitting on. For that reason, they are nearly impossible to see.

16. French Grunt *Grows to 12 in/30.5 cm*

The French grunt swims in schools, sometimes as big as a couple thousands. The school hunts together and then returns to the underwater grass beds where they sleep. French grunts are named for the sound they make when they ground their teeth.

17. Staghorn Coral

Like elkhorn coral, staghorn corals form thickets in very shallow water and provide habitat for fish. The coral gets its name from how much it looks like the antlers of a male deer. Staghorn corals are fast growing corals, but that is still only 4 inches/10 cm per year.

18. Pillar Coral

Pillar coral only exists in the Caribbean and Western Atlantic Ocean. It grows up from the sea floor and resembles fingers or columns. It is one of the few corals that can be seen feeding during the day and is a slow growing, hard coral.

19. Creole Wrasse *Grows to 12 in/30.5 cm*

The Creole wrasse changes colors as it grows. When it is young, it is almost entirely blue/purple. As a juvenile (think teenager), it changes all purple. When it is fully grown, it develops a yellow portion near its tail.

20. Southern Stingray *Grows to 5 feet across/1.5 meters*

The southern stingray is a diamond shaped whiptail stingray. It spends much of its time buried in the soft ground of the ocean with only its eyes showing. This means its mouth, which is on the bottom of its body, is facing down in the mud. It uses an electric sense to find prey.

21. Queen Angelfish *Grows to 1 ft 5 in/43.2 cm*

The queen angelfish is recognizable for the dark blue circle on its head that looks like a crown (that's how it got its name). Angelfish often swim alone or in pairs. When queen angelfish reproduce, the male and female release eggs and sperm into the water. The female can release as many as 75,000 eggs each night.

22. Lemon Shark *Grows to 11 ft/3.4 meters*

Lemon sharks live communally in shallow waters. This means they live with other lemon sharks, and liiving in a group means better communication, protection, and courting (finding a mate) behavior. After mating, lemon sharks birth live babies. Lemon sharks search at night for their prey, fish, using electroreceptors. Electroreception is the ability to feel the electric fields that other animals have around their bodies.

23. Nurse Shark *Grows to 10 ft/3 meters*

Nurse sharks are a threatened species due to human fishing. They are slow moving sharks who swim along the bottom of the ocean floor. During the day, they will rest under ledges or hang out in groups with other nurse sharks. At night, they come out alone to search in the sediment on the bottom for fish. To feed, they suck their prey into their mouths.

24. Stoplight Parrotfish *Grows to 2 ft/61 cm*

Named for the yellow spot on its tail along with its green and red/pink scales, the stoplight parrotfish is an important part of a coral reef. They primarily eat algae which they scrape off of dead coral with their parrot beak like teeth. They help keep the algae from growing too much and they poop out the crushed-up coral as sand. Believe it or not, stoplight parrotfish help create the sandy bottom of a reef.

About the Author

Megan Fitzharris is a choral music teacher, a nature lover, and an avid reader. She has been teaching music for 19 years and enjoys improvising new words to familiar songs. She also believes that it is our job to care for and preserve the Earth and all its amazing parts, such as the coral reefs. She lives in Maryland with her husband and sons, a cat, a dog, and, of course, fish.

MORE BOOKS FROM RSP PRESS

CPSIA information can be obtained
at www.ICGtesting.com
Printed in the USA
LVHW071411300321
682964LV00009B/151